The Panda

Illustrations: Marcelle Geneste
Text: Nadine Saunier

BARRON'S

New York • London • Toronto • Sydney

curls up next to his mother.

He is as light as a   ,
all white and rather fragile.
His eyes and ears look
like funny   . of black.

The young panda quickly gains  .

When he is
not turning  ,

he  trees,

explores the rhododendron bushes,

or listens to the chirp of the  .

His mother and father
are the "giant pandas."

The  lives in China,
high up on the slopes
of the mountains,

hidden in the dark .

In winter it is very ,

and the pandas frolic in the snow.

Up he goes! Papa panda settles in a huge pine tree to take a nap.

Despite his , he climbs well. This

doesn't have his own home like other animals: one night he'll sleep under a rock,

another night in a , but always well protected from his enemies — the wild dogs and the snow leopard.

The pandas are not like bears,

who ![panda sleeping] all winter long.
The panda doesn't hibernate
and must search constantly for food.
Seated with his legs apart,
he settles down and

and re-chews the leaves
and stalk of just one plant: bamboo.
He eats ten to fifteen pounds of bamboo each day.

The panda has a secret,

a 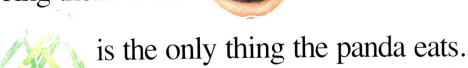 in the middle of his wrist.
This sixth finger is useful:
it allows him to break the stalks of bamboo,
peel the shoots,
and bring them to his 👄 .

🎋 is the only thing the panda eats.
It's an odd plant.
It grows, flowers once every one hundred years,
and then dies.
Many bamboo forests have been cut down.
These days, the panda has a hard time
finding enough food.

Pandas are solitary animals. But in March
or April, the male travels all around

the forest searching for a  .

Five months after the couple meets,
a tiny is born.

The mother never leaves her baby.

She  it tenderly

and with it
on a bed of bamboo stalks.
In less than a year, the baby is grown.

The young panda its mother
to lead its own life.

The panda is famous
        throughout the   .
Many visitors go to the zoo to

watch it   ,
eat bamboo leaves, or just sleep.
But pandas are endangered.
To help them survive,
reserves have been established
where people cannot go.
We hope that soon the cry of the panda,
"keng…keng,"
will echo once again in the mountain valleys.

baby panda

snow ball

splotches

weight

somersaults

climbs

birds

panda

forest

cold

weight

vagabond

cave